D0818880

Isla of Adventure

7

Marina's Turf

by Dela Costa

illustrated by Ana Sebastián

LITTLE SIMON
New York London Toronto Sydney New Delhi

If you purchased this book without a cover, you should be aware that this book is stolen property. It was reported as "unsold and destroyed" to the publisher, and neither the author nor the publisher has received any payment for this "stripped book."

This book is a work of fiction. Any references to historical events, real people, or real places are used fictitiously. Other names, characters, places, and events are products of the author's imagination, and any resemblance to actual events or places or persons, living or dead, is entirely coincidental.

LITTLE SIMON
An imprint of Simon & Schuster Children's Publishing Division
1230 Avenue of the Americas, New York, New York 10020
First Little Simon paperback edition January 2024

Series designed by Laura Roode.
Book designed by Laura Roode. The text of this book was set in Congenial.
Manufactured in the United States of America 1223 LAK
2 4 6 8 10 9 7 5 3 1
Cataloging-in-Publication Data is available for this title from the Library of Congress.
ISBN 978-1-6659-5037-4 (hc)
ISBN 978-1-6659-5036-7 (pbk)
ISBN 978-1-6659-5038-1 (ebook)

Contents

GECKO-SIZED LESSONS

◊◊◊◊◊◊◊◊◊◊◊◊◊◊

"Um . . . I think I've made a mistake," said Fitz the gecko. He was hanging onto a gecko-sized pool floatie with all his might.

On the beautiful island of Sol, the weather was perfect for the ultimate fun in the sun. The neighborhood pool was packed as kids splashed around and enjoyed the heat.

Well, except for Fitz, Isla thought.

He was trying something brand new—swimming lessons.

Though geckoes weren't natural swimmers, Fitz wasn't your average reptile. He was known for eating way too many human sweets and going on exciting adventures with Isla. Oh, and there was the fact that he and Isla could actually speak to each other.

"Honestly, I think this is your best idea yet," Isla said, smearing sunscreen all over her face, arms, and legs. She wore her favorite seashell swimsuit for this special moment.

"If you say so . . ." Fitz still looked unsure as he sat on the floatie they'd found at the Adventure Shack. They were lucky that Mama's shop had everything you could imagine in stock.

Isla finished tying her hair in a bun, then slipped into the pool's refreshing water.

"All right—listen up!" she instructed. "All you have to do is hold on tight to the floatie, then kick as fast as a hummingbird's wings! Got it?"

"Like this?" Carefully, Fitz kicked his feet.

"Even faster," Isla said. "Pretend a shark is chasing you!"

"AH!" Fitz shouted. Scrunching up his face, he kicked as quickly as he could. "I'm doing it! I'm moving! Well, I *think* I'm doing it."

Isla couldn't help but giggle. "Well . . . you're definitely doing something."

Fitz hadn't moved an inch.

"Why don't you watch me?" Isla suggested.

But before she could take off, a sound made everyone in the pool pause.

Ding! Ding! Ding!

All at once, every kid stopped what they were doing. The splashes came to a halt, and no one jumped from the diving board.

"I know that sound!" one kid gasped, taking off his goggles.

"Can it be?" a girl with floaties asked.

A woman wearing an apron rolled a metal cart into the pool area. She parked herself in the dining section, then popped open a striped umbrella attached to the cart.

"*Helado!* Ice cream!" she called out as she rang a little bell. "Come get your ice cream!"

"It's Free Ice Cream Friday!" Isla and Fitz squealed at the same time.

FLAVOR STATION

◊◊◊◊◊◊◊◊◊◊◊◊◊◊

Pineapple Party. Cool Coconut. Perfect Passion Fruit. Groovy Guava. After patiently waiting their turn, Isla and Fitz were finally at the front of the line taking a look at all the delicious ice cream flavors.

"Look at all these choices!" Fitz said, sitting on top of Isla's head for a better look. "Oooh, is that Banana Bonanza?"

He sounded out the word. “Bo-nan-za. Sounds groovy to me!”

Isla pointed to a container with lots of swirls. “This one’s new. What’s in the Sprinkle Surprise?”

The ice cream lady winked. “If I tell you, it’ll ruin the surprise!”

Fitz leaned down to look into Isla's eyes. "I can't decide!"

"How about we try one of each?" Isla asked. "Could we do that?"

"*Claro!* Of course." The ice cream lady scooped up a small serving of each flavor into two cups. She topped them off with a tiny paper umbrella.

"Here are two spoons," she said, peeking at Fitz. "One for you and one for your, ah, friend."

"My friend and I thank you!" Isla said.

She found the perfect shady spot underneath a large palm tree and gave Fitz his spoon. He crawled down eagerly to stand beside his cup, which was nearly as big as him.

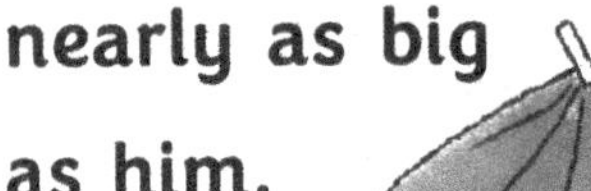

"Which should we try first?" she asked.

But Fitz had already dug in. Using his giant spoon, he scooped up some ice cream and dove in headfirst. "This . . . is . . . so . . . yummy."

Isla laughed and tried a bit of each flavor from her own cup.

"Mmm!" she said, agreeing. "Sprinkle Surprise really is surprisingly good!"

"Ice cream for lunch is always a good idea," Fitz said.

The word "lunch" made Isla's brain itch.

Lunch . . . lunch, Isla thought. *What was I supposed to do for lunch?*

Then she remembered and sprang to her feet. "Sorry to cut this short, Fitz. I totally forgot I'm supposed to meet Abuelo at the Sol Marine Rescue Center. Wanna come?"

Fitz gulped down another spoonful of ice cream. "As long as I have my ice cream, I'll follow you anywhere!"

MARINA . . . JUST MARINA

◊◊◊◊◊◊◊◊◊◊◊◊◊◊

Swooshing by on her bike, Isla pedaled straight to the Sol Marine Rescue Center, which she just called the Center.

Abuelo was a nature scientist, which meant he studied wildlife all over Sol. Today, he was at the Center studying life under the sea.

Isla swerved into the parking lot. It had a view of the sparkling ocean.

"We're heeeere!" she sang, leaning her bike against the side of the building.

"Oh, good." Fitz popped out from her bike basket, licking the last bit of Banana Bonanza off his face. "Believe it or not, I'm ready for lunch."

"You're ALWAYS ready for lunch," Isla joked.

As they walked in, she couldn't help but admire the Center's lobby. Even though they were inside, it still smelled like salty sea air. Fish nets hung from the ceiling, ocean-inspired paintings decorated the walls, and starfish were painted on the front desk.

Miss Moreno typed away on her computer. She helped visitors find their way.

"Isla, *hola*!" she said. "Your abuelo said you'd be stopping by today. You're in for a surprise."

"A surprise?" Isla echoed.

In her shirt pocket, Fitz sighed. "Well, there goes lunch."

"Did you hear about this morning's rescue?" Miss Moreno asked.

Isla's heart skipped a beat. "A rescue? Here? Right now? Today?"

Of course, she *hadn't* heard about it. If she had, she would've been here first thing in the morning!

Miss Moreno filled out a visitor's pass. "Why don't you check it out? You'll find your abuelo by the pools."

"Thanks!" Isla stuck the pass to her shirt, then rushed down the hall. She hurried past the labs, the offices, and the supply room.

Fitz started to look a little green. "Slow down, Isla. You're making a milkshake in my tummy."

"Hold it in, bud!" Isla said. "I've got to *sea* who Abuelo rescued. Get it? *Sea?*"

Fitz groaned. "*Very* funny."

She reached the back of the building and pushed open a door, revealing a large space with multiple pools. A tarp covered the area, so the water wouldn't get too hot. Isla weaved among the pools, peeking in a few to see some animal friends.

"Isla!" a voice called. "Over here!"

Abuelo and Mr. Vet stood near a giant pool all in the way in the back.

Mr. Vet was Sol's favorite veterinarian. That wasn't *actually* his name, but it's what Isla had called him since she was little, and it had stuck.

"Ugh." Fitz shivered on her shoulder. "The vet . . ."

Isla raised an eyebrow. "Fitz, you're a wild gecko. You've never been to the vet."

The gecko crossed his arms. "And I hope I never do."

When she reached him, Abuelo gave Isla a warm hug. "Perfect timing!"

"It's been too long since you volunteered at the vet clinic," Mr. Vet said, shaking her hand. "And you too, Fitz."

Fitz hid in Isla's hair.

"I heard you found a new friend today," Isla said.

"Yeah, *we* did," a new, unexpected voice said. "But who are *you*?"

A boy Isla's age stepped out from behind Mr. Vet. He wore one of the Center's volunteer shirts and an upside-down smile.

Mr. Vet gave the boy a gentle pat on the shoulder. "Have you two never met? This is my nephew."

"You two get to know each other while we go grab our notes," Abuelo said.

As the grown-ups left, Isla reached out a hand. "Pleasure to meet you! I'm—"

"Isla Verde," the boy interrupted. "Yeah, I've heard all about you. You're the girl who has animal friends."

Fitz scoffed into Isla's ear. "He says it like it's a bad thing!"

"I'm Luca Marina, but you can just call me Marina," the boy continued. "And *I'm* the one who's here to help the baby dolphin."

LOST IN TRANSLATION

◊◊◊◊◊◊◊◊◊◊◊◊◊◊◊

Isla realized a few things at once.

The first was that her hand was still reaching for a handshake that wasn't going to come. She quickly dropped it.

The second was that this boy—Marina—totally did *not* want her to help.

And the third was—

"Did you say you found a baby dolphin?" Isla gasped.

"That's right," Marina said. "You can look, I guess, but try not to startle her."

Lowering herself to her knees, Isla peered over the pool to get a better look. Sure enough, she spotted a baby dolphin curled up in the far bottom corner.

"I've never seen a dolphin act like such a sad puppy," Fitz said. "Or stay so still."

He was right. Dolphins are known to be playful creatures, not quiet ones.

"She doesn't seem to be hurt, so we're still trying to understand what's wrong with her," Marina said with a know-it-all air. "She was crying out near the shore this morning. Your grandpa knew it would be best to bring her to the Center, so she wouldn't be all alone."

"Don't worry, girl," Isla said reassuringly into the water. "You're safe here."

As soon as Isla's words made it through the water, the dolphin looked up and swam to the surface. She broke through the water in a graceful arc, then splashed back under.

"Whoa!" Isla, Fitz, and Marina cried out in surprise as water splashed them.

Isla giggled as she wiped away drops from her face. The dolphin poked her head out of the water.

Eeee! Eeee! Eeee!

Marina knelt by Isla. His eyes narrowed in suspicion. "What gives, Verde? How did you do that?"

"Do what?" Isla asked.

"You know what," Marina said. "The dolphin came up here almost as if you'd called her!"

Isla gulped. *That's a little too close to the truth. He doesn't need to know about my animal-speaking secret.*

Eeee! Eeee! the dolphin squealed.

"What is it?" Isla asked. "What do you need?"

Eeee! Eeee!

But for the first time ever, Isla didn't understand what one of her animal friends was trying to tell her. In fact, she couldn't make out a single word.

CHAPTER 5

DOLPHIN-ITELY PUZZLED

Abuelo and Mr. Vet returned just then, cheering as they realized the dolphin was finally out of hiding.

"This is incredible!" Mr. Vet said. "Now we can find out what's really wrong with our new friend. Great work, kids!"

"Oh, we should get into the water," Abuelo said. "Marina, Isla—could you grab vests for us?"

Suddenly, Marina cheered up. "Yes, we can! Come along, Verde."

Still surprised that she couldn't understand the dolphin, Isla followed Marina into the building in a confused daze.

"Isla?" Fitz asked. "Are you okay?"

"I don't understand," she whispered. "I've spoken to dolphins before. They even taught me how to swim!"

The sudden feeling of warm sunlight as she stepped out of the Center made her pause. Confused, she turned to see Marina still standing inside the building, holding the door open.

"Um." She looked left and right. "Are the vests out here now?"

"Don't worry about that." Marina crossed his arms. "Why don't you leave all the sea stuff to me, and you go about your day?"

"But I said I would help," Isla argued.

"I'll tell your Abuelo you had to go play with earthworms or something!" He waved goodbye before disappearing. "See ya!"

The Center doors shut, leaving Isla standing outside.

"Hey, check this out!" Fitz said proudly, splashing his little feet in the water.

Back in the neighborhood pool, Fitz was finally able to move back and forth on his floatie. Isla floated on her back beside him, staring up at the passing clouds.

"Great job, pal," Isla replied without looking.

Ever since leaving the Center, she'd been trying to make sense of this dolphin mystery. She was even seeing dolphin-shaped clouds.

Why couldn't Isla understand the sea creature? And how come Marina was so bossy?

"Oooh, look at this!" Fitz called out. "See how I'm using my tail to help push myself forward? It's too bad humans don't have one."

"Uh-huh," Isla muttered.

Fitz zoomed by her head. "Should we get more ice cream? I want to try the Stinkbug flavor."

"Sounds good." Isla dipped her finger in the water and swirled it around.

"I knew it!" Fitz pulled himself onto the floatie and splashed water her way. "You're distracted! You know that Stinkbug is the worst ice cream flavor ever!"

"Oh, I'm sorry, Fitz," Isla said, guiltily. She stood up. "I don't mean to be distracted. It's just . . ."

"It's just that you really want to help the dolphin," Fitz finished for her. "We should go back! After all, I'm a pro swimmer now."

"I'm very proud of you." Isla gave him a high five. "But what about Marina?"

"What about him?" Fitz shrugged. "When has anyone stopped you from helping an animal in need? You're Isla Verde!"

Isla cracked a smile. “You’re right. We’ve got a dolphin to help!”

“That’s the spirit.” Fitz tried to stand, but his sticky fingers wouldn’t budge. “But first help me out of this floatie. I think I’m stuck!”

ALARM WORDS

◆◆◆◆◆◆◆◆◆◆◆◆◆◆

Isla snuck back into the Sol Marine Rescue Center with one goal in mind. No matter what, she had to avoid Marina at all costs.

As she snuck through the halls, Isla peered around corners and tried to keep quiet.

"All right, Fitz," she whispered. "Keep your eyes open for not-so-friendly kids."

Fitz's eyes became impossibly large. "These peepers are not shutting! Ooh, are those fresh bananas in the lunch room?"

"Fitz!" Isla said. "Focus!"

The gecko shook his head fiercely. "Right, right! How about I come up with an alarm word for if I see Marina strutting around? You know, like a real spy."

Isla tiptoed past another room. "Good idea."

"How about . . . bananas?" Fitz said, then changed his mind. "No, no, that would be confusing because I always talk about bananas. Oh, how about berries? No, let's use ice cream! What do you think about star fruit?"

As Fitz thought about his alarm word, Isla made it to the outside pools without a hitch. Luckily, no one was around. Isla could have all the time in the world to figure out why she couldn't understand her new friend.

The dolphin was once again hiding in the bottom corner of the pool.

Isla kneeled down and waved. "*Psst.* Over here!"

At her call, the dolphin eagerly swam to the surface. *Eeee! Eeee!*

Isla gently patted the dolphin's nose. "It's good to see you too."

The dolphin splashed around the pool and called out again, but Isla still had no idea what she was saying. Underwater creatures spoke a little differently than animals who lived on land. Each time they spoke, a bubble popped between each word. Isla gave it a shot.

"How—*POP!* Are—*POP!* You?" Isla asked, making sure to make the popping sounds extra loud.

The dolphin tilted her head.

"Ugh, it's no use!" Isla groaned.

The dolphin swam off again, this time back to her corner.

"It's like trying to speak to an actual baby," Fitz said, observing. "This one time, my cousin tried speaking to a baby gecko but couldn't understand a single thing that little hatchling was squeaking."

"Really?" Isla's eyes widened.

"Yep. Babies speak weirdly," Fitz said. "Actually, they don't really speak at all. They just make up words."

Isla gazed thoughtfully at the dolphin. *Could it be that I can't understand you because you're too young?*

Suddenly, Fitz shot into the air and shouted in horror. "BANANAS! BERRIES! ICE CREAM! STAR FRUIT! ALL THE FRUITS!"

"Fitz, are you still hungry?" Isla asked.

"The alarm words!" he hissed.

A shadow loomed over them as a suspicious voice asked, "What are you doing back here, Verde?"

Isla turned to see a crossed-armed Marina.

Uh-oh. We're caught dolphin-handed.

THINK FAST!

◊◊◊◊◊◊◊◊◊◊◊◊◊◊◊◊

What do you do when someone catches you somewhere they don't want you to be? Distract them until you can run away!

Isla shot up to her feet and didn't know what to do with her hands. "Hi! We didn't see you—I mean, *I* didn't see you there. How are you? Good? Cool! Oh, what am I doing here, you ask? That's a great question!"

Marina blinked. "Those are a lot of words all at once."

Fitz covered his eyes. "This is too awkward to watch!"

Taking a deep breath, Isla began again. She straightened up her back and looked Marina right in the eyes. "I know that you know a lot about the ocean, and that's so cool! But I also know a lot about animals. I think if we work together, we can help this dolphin. What do you say? Should we join our *fin*-tastic minds?"

For a moment, Marina said nothing. Then he asked, "What kind of animal is a dolphin?"

Fitz slumped over. "Oh, joy . . . a quiz."

"They're mammals," Isla replied confidently. "To be more specific, this one is a bottlenose dolphin."

Eeee! Eeee! The dolphin cheered, splashing back to the surface.

Marina went on with his questions. "Do you think animals are just as smart as humans?"

Isla snorted. "Of course! This little one here is smarter, actually. She has a bigger brain than you."

"Oh, burn!" Fitz pretended to blow smoke from his finger.

Isla jumped, realizing her mistake. "I meant dolphins have bigger brains than *all* humans. Even me. Not just you."

Marina narrowed his eyes. "One last question, Verde. The hardest one yet. How many stomachs do dolphins have?"

Isla brightened. "They have one stomach—"

"HA!" Marina threw his hands up in victory. "Wrong!"

"I wasn't finished yet," Isla said. "They have one stomach, *plus* an extra one to store their food."

"I wish I had TWO stomachs," Fitz said. "Imagine how many more snacks I could eat."

Marina looked surprised. A smile slowly spread across his face. "It seems you *do* know your stuff, Verde. Maybe I judged you too harshly."

"The past is in the past," Isla said. "Now, what do you say we help out this little one?"

Marina stuck his hand out for a shake. "Welcome aboard!"

SEA BRAINS AT WORK

◊◊◊◊◊◊◊◊◊◊◊◊◊◊

A shared love for animals wasn't the only thing Marina and Isla had in common. He also kept an adventure notepad.

He pulled it out of his pocket and flipped to a page filled with notes and drawings. Where Isla typically drew land creatures, Marina's drawings were all about life under the sea. There were seaweed, whales, coral, crabs, and even sharks.

“Whoa!” Isla peered at his shark notes. “Have you met a great white shark before?”

“Only one time,” Marina said. “You know, they’re not really as mean as everyone thinks. Just don’t swim too close to them. They like their space.”

"Have you always loved the ocean?" Isla asked.

Marina turned a little red and scratched his neck. "Pretty much. I grew up in a beach house just off Canto Coast. That's why I know there are a few reasons animals hide like our friend here. The first is that they're injured and need time alone to heal."

"But we didn't find an injury on her," Isla pointed out.

Marina lifted another finger. "The second reason is that she could be shy in this new place."

They looked into the pool, where the dolphin swam back and forth deep in the water.

"She seems more sad than shy," Isla said.

Marina flipped through his notes. "That could be true."

But what could she be so sad about if she's not hurt? Isla wondered.

She thought about how the dolphin was found crying and all alone. If she wasn't calling out for human help, there was just one other explanation.

"What if she was searching for someone?" Isla asked. "What if she was looking for her family? She's too young to be all alone, right?"

Marina snapped his fingers. "That's genius, Verde!"

Isla leapt up to her feet. "If there's a dolphin pod swimming around Sol, Abuelo will know all about it. Come on."

Isla, Fitz, and Marina rushed back into the Center and to Abuelo's office. The room was filled with books, papers, and maps of oceans all over the world.

"Abuelo!" Isla exclaimed. "We have answers that need questions! I mean, we have questions that need answers!"

Abuelo looked up from his work. "How can I help?"

"Verde here figured out that the dolphin might be separated from her pod," Marina explained. "Have you tracked any groups lately?"

"A pod, you say?" Abuelo hummed thoughtfully, stood up from his desk, and walked over to a map of Sol on the wall. It was marked up with all sorts of circles and Xs, dotted lines, and notes. He pointed to a large circle in the water near the Center. "We found her here. And this pod I've been tracking usually swims right about . . . here." He pointed to another circle, which was just a few miles off. "I've never seen a baby dolphin traveling with this group before, but it's possible I completely missed her."

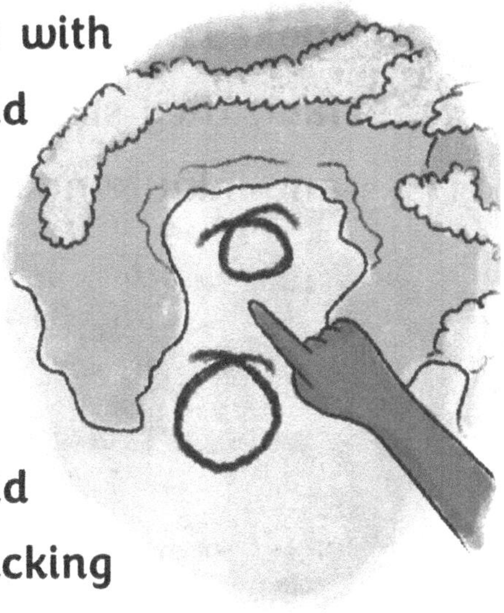

"Will they be back soon?" Isla asked.

"According to their swimming patterns, they should be back . . ." He looked at a clock on the wall. "Today! In fact, they should be reaching the shore any minute now."

Marina groaned. “Oh no! What if we don’t catch them in time?”

Isla balled her hands into fists, determination coursing through her. “We will totally make it in time! Right, Abuelo?”

Abuelo grabbed a pair of keys from his desk. “We’d better start the boat!”

NEW FRIENDS

◊◊◊◊◊◊◊◊◊◊◊◊◊◊◊◊

While Abuelo prepared a small boat on the Center's dock, Isla and Marina stopped by the supply room. It was filled with all sorts of marine equipment, including the life vests they needed for the mission.

Marina dug around in a bin, then tossed a red vest to Isla. "Here—this one should fit."

Isla slipped it on. "Thanks!"

"Um, this doesn't have pockets," Fitz whispered. "Where do I fit?"

"You might have to stay on the boat with Abuelo," Isla whispered back.

Marina turned around with his own vest on. "What was that?"

"Oh, nothing!" Isla said sheepishly. "Just talking to myself. I do that a lot."

After looking between Isla and Fitz suspiciously, Marina shrugged. "It's okay that you speak to animals, you know. I do it all the time."

Isla gasped. "You do?"

"Yeah!" Marina said, then laughed. "It's not like they speak back, though."

"Oh, right!" Isla replied awkwardly. "That would be so, uh, wild."

Marina looked down at his feet. "Hey, Verde? I wanted to say that I'm sorry for not being very nice to you earlier. I can be a little protective over the ocean and all that. For what it's worth, I don't really think you look for earthworms all day."

Isla grinned. "I actually do look for earthworms a lot of the time. They're so silly!"

Marina laughed.

Together, they headed out to the dock where Abuelo waited in the motorboat. They climbed on, Abuelo pushed on a lever, and they were off into the glittering blue water.

"Wait a minute," Fitz said. "Aren't we forgetting the dolphin? You know, the whole reason we're here?"

"Over there!" Isla pointed to the shore, where Mr. Vet and Miss Moreno were lowering a large tarp. The baby

dolphin lay in it patiently. Little by little, she was lowered into the sea. She pushed forward and splashed into the water with a happy cry.

Eeee! Eeee!

"Woo-hoo!" Marina cheered.

When they reached a safe distance from the shore, Abuelo anchored the boat.

Isla ran from side to side, searching for fins sticking up from the water. "See anything?"

"No sign yet!" Abuelo replied. "But you might get a better view in the water. It's the perfect area to dive in safely."

"Diving? Into the sea?" Fitz hopped down from Isla's shoulder and landed on the side of the boat. "I'll stick to pools."

"Ready?" Marina asked Isla.

They counted down. "Three . . . two . . . ONE!"

BLUE, BRIGHT, AND BEAUTIFUL

◊◊◊◊◊◊◊◊◊◊◊◊◊◊

Splash!

The cool water around Isla bubbled as she jumped in. Thanks to her life vest, she floated right back to the top. Beside her, Marina swam in circles.

"Doesn't the water feel great?" he asked. "I wish I could live in the ocean."

"Let's look under," Isla said.

They held in their breath and stuck

their heads into the water. It took Isla's eyes a moment to open and take in the beauty underneath.

A school of striped fish swam by, then a group of blue fish, and then a few spotted fish, too. The sand glittered with

tiny shells. A crab crawled by, waving a claw. Even a turtle soared beside Isla, then grazed through the sand for seaweed.

Everything was blue, bright, and beautiful.

Marina tapped Isla on the arm excitedly and pointed forward. It was the baby dolphin swimming toward them!

"Hi!" Isla gasped with delight.

"We thought you were gone!" Marina added.

Eeee! Eeee!

"She sure *eees* at you a lot. Maybe we should start calling you Isla Verde-*eee-eee*!" Marina joked.

"Kids! Here they come!" Abuelo called from the boat.

A pod of six dolphins splashed in and out of the water, calling loudly as they swam forward. The baby dolphin squealed with excitement and swam off in a hurry to meet them.

Isla watched joyfully as they were reunited. Just when she thought the moment couldn't get any better, one of the bigger dolphins swam up to her.

"This must be her mom!" Isla said.

Carefully, the dolphin gently touched her nose to Isla's. "Thank-*POP!*-you!"

To Marina, it must have sounded like a bunch of pops.

"You're—*POP!*—welcome," Isla replied.

The dolphins all dove underwater, then splashed out in beautiful arcs as they swam away.

"You can communicate very well with animals," Marina said. He gave Isla a funny look. "It's almost like you know what they're saying."

Isla giggled, waving at the dolphins. "You have no idea."

DON'T MISS ISLA'S NEXT ADVENTURE!

HERE'S A SNEAK PEEK!

Isla Verde typically began her days with a few important tasks.

The first task was brushing her hair and teeth at the same time. This way, both chores went by faster.

Next, Isla made her bed with one quick pull of her blankets. Her gecko best friend, Fitz, helped by fluffing the pillow.

After that, Mama always whipped up a delicious breakfast for all three of them.

But today, things were running a bit differently in the Verde house.

This time, Isla wasn't following her usual routine. This time, she was getting ready for her biggest adventure yet.

Today, Isla was going on her first-ever airplane ride! All she had left to do before leaving the house was close her suitcase. But it turned out that filling it with clothes, books, and lots of adventure gear was making it a bit difficult to zip up.

Fitz watched from the couch as Isla fought with the zipper. "You're not moving to La Ciudad, you know. You crammed too much in there!" he said.

La Ciudad—the big city. It's where

Mama had grown up, where Isla's friend Tora had moved from, and the one place Isla was most curious about.

"Crammed too much? No such thing!" Isla declared. Using both her hands, she tried to force the suitcase shut. "This old thing just needs . . . a little . . . push!"

"Allow me!" Fitz said. With one great gecko leap, he landed on the suitcase.

With the weight of her hands and Fitz's hops, the zipper finally gave in.

Ziiiiiiiiiip!

Isla high-fived her friend. "This suitcase is as snug as a bug."

Fitz tilted his head. "Do you think you'll find bugs in La Ciudad? What if they're different from the ones here? What if they're super giant?"

Isla thought about it. The big city was, well, big.

"I haven't read anything about giant city bugs," Isla said, then gave Fitz a sad look. "But I do wish you could come find out with me."

Geckos weren't allowed on airplanes. It was the greatest bummer in the whole world.

"Me? In the sky? Hundreds of feet above the ground?" Fitz shivered. "That's no place for a gecko. You'll just have to draw everything you see and show me when you get back."

"It's a done deal," Isla promised.